MAD LIBS®

SCOOBY-DOO MYSTERY MAD LIBS

By Roger Price and Leonard Stern

PSS!
PRICE STERN SLOAN

ISBN 0-8431-0239-X

First Edition
1 3 5 7 9 10 8 6 4 2

MAD LIBS ®

MAD LIBS® is a game for people who don't like games!
It can be played by one, two, three, four, or forty.

• RIDICULOUSLY SIMPLE DIRECTIONS

In this tablet you will find stories containing blank spaces where words are left out. One player, the READER, selects one of these stories. The READER does not tell anyone what the story is about. Instead, he/she asks the other players, the WRITERS, to give him/her words. These words are used to fill in the blank spaces in the story.

• TO PLAY

The READER asks each WRITER in turn to call out a word—an adjective or a noun or whatever the space calls for—and uses them to fill in the blank spaces in the story. The result is a MAD LIBS® game.

When the READER then reads the completed MAD LIBS® game to the other players, they will discover that they have written a story that is fantastic, screamingly funny, shocking, silly, crazy, or just plain dumb—depending upon which words each WRITER called out.

• EXAMPLE (*Before* and *After*)

"_____!" he said _____
         EXCLAMATION   ADVERB

as he jumped into his convertible _____ and
                                                      NOUN

drove off with his _____ wife.
                            ADJECTIVE

"*Ouch!*_____!" he said *stupidly*_____
       EXCLAMATION   ADVERB

as he jumped into his convertible *cat*_____ and
                                            NOUN

drove off with his *brave*_____ wife.
                        ADJECTIVE

MAD LIBS®

In case you have forgotten what adjectives, adverbs, nouns, and verbs are, here is a quick review:

An ADJECTIVE describes something or somebody. *Lumpy, soft, ugly, messy,* and *short* are adjectives.

An ADVERB tells how something is done. It modifies a verb and usually ends in "ly." *Modestly, stupidly, greedily,* and *carefully* are adverbs.

A NOUN is the name of a person, place or thing. *Sidewalk, umbrella, bridle, bathtub,* and *nose* are nouns.

A VERB is an action word. *Run, pitch, jump,* and *swim* are verbs. Put the verbs in past tense if the directions say PAST TENSE. *Ran, pitched, jumped,* and *swam* are verbs in the past tense.

When we ask for a PLACE, we mean any sort of place: a country or city *(Spain, Cleveland)* or a room *(bathroom, kitchen.)*

An EXCLAMATION or SILLY WORD is any sort of funny sound, gasp, grunt, or outcry, like *Wow!, Ouch!, Whomp!, Ick!,* and *Gadzooks!*

When we ask for specific words, like a NUMBER, a COLOR, an ANIMAL, or a PART OF THE BODY, we mean a word that is one of those things, like *seven, blue, horse,* or *head*.

When we ask for a PLURAL, it means more than one. For example, *cat* pluralized is *cats*.

MAD LIBS® is fun to play with friends, but you can also play it by yourself! To begin with, DO NOT look at the story on the page below. Fill in the blanks on this page with the words called for. Then, using the words you have selected, fill in the blank spaces in the story.

Now you've created your own hilarious MAD LIBS® game!

SHERLOCK BONES IN THE HOUND OF THE BASKETBALLS, PART 1

ADJECTIVE_____

OCCUPATION _____

TYPE OF BUILDING _____

ADJECTIVE_____

VERB ENDING IN "ING" _____

ROOM _____

SILLY WORD_____

A PLACE _____

ANIMAL _____

ADJECTIVE_____

It was a dark and _____ night, and Scooby-Doo, the world's
                          ADJECTIVE

greatest _____ , was at home relaxing with his good friend
              OCCUPATION

Dr. Shaggy Watson, in their _____ on Baker Street.
                                 TYPE OF BUILDING

They had just finished solving the _____ case of the
                                          ADJECTIVE

_____ Men and were glad to be home again. Just then,
 VERB ENDING IN "ING"

there was a knock on the door to the _____ . "_____,"
                                          ROOM   SILLY WORD

a voice said. "I would like a chance to talk to you about a mystery,

Sherlock Bones." Shaggy opened the door, and in walked Fred the

Count of _____ ."Please come in," said Shaggy. "Ri'm Rerrock
             A PLACE

Rones, rut rou ran rall re Scooby-Doo." The Count explained that his

home, Basketball Hall, was haunted by a giant _____." We
                                                        ANIMAL

are completely _____ and don't know where else to turn.
                     ADJECTIVE

Will you help me, Scooby-Doo?" he asked.

MAD LIBS® is fun to play with friends, but you can also play it by yourself! To begin with, DO NOT look at the story on the page below. Fill in the blanks on this page with the words called for. Then, using the words you have selected, fill in the blank spaces in the story.

Now you've created your own hilarious MAD LIBS® game!

SHERLOCK BONES IN THE HOUND OF THE BASKETBALLS, PART 2

ADJECTIVE_____

ADVERB_____

ARTICLE OF CLOTHING (PLURAL)_____

NOUN _____

ADJECTIVE_____

ADJECTIVE_____

SILLY WORD_____

NUMBER _____

PLURAL NOUN _____

SAME ANIMAL AS IN PART 1 _____

ADJECTIVE_____

PLURAL NOUN _____

VERB (PAST TENSE)_____

ADVERB_____

MAD LIBS®
SHERLOCK BONES IN THE HOUND
OF THE BASKETBALLS, PART 2

Scooby-Doo and Shaggy arrived at _____ Basketball Hall
                                        ADJECTIVE

_____ the next morning. They were greeted at the door by
   ADVERB

Fred's loyal servant, Daphne. "Come in, come in," she said. She took

their _____ and hung them on the _____
        ARTICLE OF CLOTHING (PLURAL)   NOUN

next to the door. "The Count will be _____ to hear you've
                                            ADJECTIVE

arrived. We really are getting _____ with worry over this
                                      ADJECTIVE

creature." Then Fred met them and started to show them around the

grounds. "Here's the place where my Great Uncle _____
                                                       SILLY WORD

signed the deed to Basketball Hall, over _____ years ago," he
                                              NUMBER

explained. They walked a little further to a grove of _____ .
                                                         PLURAL NOUN

"And here's the place where the _____ appears
                                   SAME ANIMAL AS IN PART 1

every night." Just then, they heard a/an _____ sound— like
                                               ADJECTIVE

two _____ being _____ . "Oh, no, it's the creature!"
     PLURAL NOUN   VERB (PAST TENSE)

Fred said _____ .
             ADVERB

MAD LIBS® is fun to play with friends, but you can also play it by yourself! To begin with, DO NOT look at the story on the page below. Fill in the blanks on this page with the words called for. Then, using the words you have selected, fill in the blank spaces in the story.

Now you've created your own hilarious MAD LIBS® game!

SHERLOCK BONES IN THE HOUND OF THE BASKETBALLS, PART 3

ADVERB_____

PART OF THE BODY (PLURAL) _____

VERB _____

ADJECTIVE_____

VERB ENDING IN "ING" _____

PART OF THE BODY _____

ARTICLE OF CLOTHING_____

PERSON IN ROOM _____

TYPE OF BUILDING _____

SAME PERSON IN ROOM_____

ADVERB_____

ADJECTIVE_____

_____, the creature came closer and closer. Scooby and Shaggy

ADVERB

were shaking so hard, their _____ were knocking

PART OF THE BODY (PLURAL)

together. "Raggy," Scooby said, "R'im rared." Shaggy answered, "Like, I

know, Scooby. I'm so scared I think I might _____." The

VERB

creature came closer and closer. Fred started to hide behind Shaggy

and Scooby, as if they would protect him from the _____

ADJECTIVE

monster in front of them. The monster came closer. It was howling

and _____. All of a sudden, Shaggy stopped and

VERB ENDING IN "ING"

lunged at the monster. "Like, this isn't a monster, Fred. Someone just

wants you to think it is." He reached out and pulled on the monster's

_____ as hard as he could. Its _____ popped

PART OF THE BODY   ARTICLE OF CLOTHING

off and revealed the face of _____ , hiding

PERSON IN ROOM

inside. "I wanted to knock down Basketball Hall and build a/an

_____," _____ said _____. "Now my

TYPE OF BUILDING SAME PERSON IN ROOM   ADVERB

plans have been ruined and are _____ , thanks to

ADJECTIVE

the great detective, Sherlock Bones."

MAD LIBS® is fun to play with friends, but you can also play it by yourself! To begin with, DO NOT look at the story on the page below. Fill in the blanks on this page with the words called for. Then, using the words you have selected, fill in the blank spaces in the story.

Now you've created your own hilarious MAD LIBS® game!

HOW TO BE A DETECTIVE

ADJECTIVE_____

NUMBER _____

CELEBRITY _____

FAMOUS CHARACTER_____

VERB ENDING IN "ING" _____

PLURAL NOUN _____

ANOTHER PLURAL NOUN_____

ADJECTIVE_____

ADJECTIVE_____

ADVERB_____

TYPE OF FOOD (PLURAL) _____

OCCUPATION _____

MAD LIBS
HOW TO BE A DETECTIVE

If you want to make your career by being a/an _____ detective,
ADJECTIVE

there are some tips you should know, according to Scooby-Doo and

his pals, who have been solving crimes for over _____ years.
NUMBER

- Start by reading lots of books and magazines by _____ .
CELEBRITY

He/She has played the part of _____ the detective
FAMOUS CHARACTER

so many times, it comes as naturally as _____ .
VERB ENDING IN "ING"

- Tell your friends that you are very good at finding things like

lost _____ and _____ . They can get
PLURAL NOUN   ANOTHER PLURAL NOUN

the word out to people who might be looking for someone

with your skills.

- When you are hired, be sure to ask lots of _____
ADJECTIVE

questions and look for plenty of _____ clues. These
ADJECTIVE

will help you _____ solve the crime.
ADVERB

- Make sure you have a good supply of _____
TYPE OF FOOD (PLURAL)

on hand, for the greatest _____ dog of all, Scooby-Doo!
OCCUPATION

MAD LIBS® is fun to play with friends, but you can also play it by yourself! To begin with, DO NOT look at the story on the page below. Fill in the blanks on this page with the words called for. Then, using the words you have selected, fill in the blank spaces in the story.

Now you've created your own hilarious MAD LIBS® game!

THE MUSEUM MYSTERY, PART 1

ADJECTIVE_____

GEOGRAPHICAL LOCATION _____

OCCUPATION _____

ADJECTIVE_____

ROOM _____

NOUN _____

ADJECTIVE_____

ADVERB_____

ADJECTIVE_____

NOUN _____

ADJECTIVE_____

MAD LIBS®
THE MUSEUM MYSTERY, PART 1

The Scooby gang had been invited to the _____ opening of
ADJECTIVE

the National Museum in _____ . When they got to
GEOGRAPHICAL LOCATION

the museum, Dr. Gutierrez, its head _____ , took them on
OCCUPATION

a/an _____ tour. "Here we have the _____ , and
ADJECTIVE   ROOM

through here, we have the only complete skeleton of a _____
NOUN

in existence," he explained. Scooby-Doo gazed up at the _____
ADJECTIVE

fossil. "Runch!" he barked. "No, Scooby," Dr. Gutierrez said _____ ,
ADVERB

"You don't want those bones. A legend says they are haunted by the

ghost of a dead dinosaur." Just then, there was a/an _____
ADJECTIVE

crashing sound, like a very large _____ being dropped. "Like,
NOUN

it's the ghost!" said Shaggy. "There's no such things as ghosts," Velma

said, "but I'll bet there is a/an _____ mystery to be solved!"
ADJECTIVE

MAD LIBS® is fun to play with friends, but you can also play it by yourself! To begin with, DO NOT look at the story on the page below. Fill in the blanks on this page with the words called for. Then, using the words you have selected, fill in the blank spaces in the story.

Now you've created your own hilarious MAD LIBS® game!

THE MUSEUM MYSTERY, PART 2

PLURAL NOUN _____

VERB _____

ROOM _____

NOUN _____

ADVERB _____

NOUN _____

SAME ROOM _____

ANOTHER ROOM _____

PLURAL NOUN _____

VERB _____

Fred and Daphne decided that they would look for _____ in

PLURAL NOUN

the upstairs part of the museum. Velma decided to _____

VERB

in the dinosaur area, and Scooby-Doo and Shaggy went to tackle the

museum's _____ , so that they could get a snack if they needed

ROOM

one. As they were wandering around the upper level of the museum,

Fred and Daphne came across a giant _____ . "This might be a

NOUN

clue," Fred said. "You're right," said Daphne _____ . "But what does

ADVERB

it mean? I'm pretty sure the museum isn't haunted by a _____ ,

NOUN

like Dr. Gutierrez says, but what's he hiding?" Meanwhile, Scooby and

Shaggy found their way to the _____ . It took them a while,

SAME ROOM

because they got lost and ended up in _____ instead. "Hey,

ANOTHER ROOM

Scoob," Shaggy said, pointing to a pile of _____ , "like, this must

PLURAL NOUN

be one of the clues!" At the same time, Velma uncovered the secret

behind the ghost. But before she could find the others, she tripped

and started to _____ into a hole in the floor of the museum!

VERB

MAD LIBS® is fun to play with friends, but you can also play it by yourself! To begin with, DO NOT look at the story on the page below. Fill in the blanks on this page with the words called for. Then, using the words you have selected, fill in the blank spaces in the story.

Now you've created your own hilarious MAD LIBS® game!

THE MUSEUM MYSTERY, PART 3

ROOM _____

ADJECTIVE _____

ADJECTIVE _____

PLURAL NOUN _____

SILLY WORD _____

PLURAL NOUN _____

VERB _____

COLOR _____

A PLACE _____

NOUN _____

ANOTHER PLACE _____

ADVERB _____

ADJECTIVE _____

NOUN _____

NUMBER _____

ANOTHER NUMBER _____

ADJECTIVE _____

MAD LIBS®
THE MUSEUM MYSTERY, PART 3

Velma had landed in the museum's _____ . It was a/an _____
ROOM · ADJECTIVE

and _____ space, full of boxes that were labeled
ADJECTIVE

" _____ " and others that were marked with stickers that
PLURAL NOUN

said, " _____ : *Handle With Care.*" "This must be where the
SILLY WORD

museum stores all its unused _____," Velma said to herself.
PLURAL NOUN

She found a light and started to _____ through the boxes. She
VERB

found a _____ statue with a label that said it was from
COLOR

_____ and an antique _____ from _____ , but as she
A PLACE · NOUN · ANOTHER PLACE

_____ came around the corner, she saw the most _____
ADVERB · ADJECTIVE

_____ she had ever seen. It was over _____ feet tall and
NOUN · NUMBER

at least _____ feet wide. And, most importantly, it was
ANOTHER NUMBER

capable of making the _____ noises they had heard earlier!
ADJECTIVE

MAD LIBS® is fun to play with friends, but you can also play it by yourself! To begin with, DO NOT look at the story on the page below. Fill in the blanks on this page with the words called for. Then, using the words you have selected, fill in the blank spaces in the story.

Now you've created your own hilarious MAD LIBS® game!

THE MUSEUM MYSTERY, PART 4

VERB (PAST TENSE)_____

NOUN _____

ADJECTIVE_____

SAME NOUN_____

NOUN _____

ADJECTIVE_____

ADVERB_____

VERB _____

ROOM _____

PLURAL NOUN _____

ADVERB_____

SAME PLURAL NOUN _____

ADJECTIVE_____

ADJECTIVE_____

MAD LIBS®
THE MUSEUM MYSTERY, PART 4

Velma found the stairs and _____ back to the main gallery,
                              VERB (PAST TENSE)

where she met Daphne and Fred, who told her about the _____
                                                         NOUN

that they had seen in the upper levels of the museum. She told them

about the _____ things she had seen in the basement. "Some-
            ADJECTIVE

one must use the _____ as a costume. Then they use the giant
                  SAME NOUN

_____ from the basement to make those _____ noises,"
  NOUN   ADJECTIVE

Velma said _____ . "But why are they trying to _____
            ADVERB   VERB

people?" Fred asked. Just then Scooby-Doo and Shaggy came in. "Like,

you would not believe what we found in the _____ . It was a stack
                                            ROOM

of _____ as tall as Scooby-Doo!" Shaggy said, as Dr. Gutierrez
   PLURAL NOUN

_____ walked into the room. "So, you have found me out! I wanted
ADVERB

the _____ for myself, and I would have gotten away with
    SAME PLURAL NOUN

it, if it weren't for you _____ kids and your _____ dog!"
                          ADJECTIVE   ADJECTIVE

MAD LIBS® is fun to play with friends, but you can also play it by yourself! To begin with, DO NOT look at the story on the page below. Fill in the blanks on this page with the words called for. Then, using the words you have selected, fill in the blank spaces in the story.

Now you've created your own hilarious MAD LIBS® game!

WHAT'S FOR DINNER, SCOOBY-DOO?

ADVERB _____

NOUN _____

PLURAL NOUN _____

TYPE OF FOOD (PLURAL) _____

VERB ENDING IN "ING" _____

TYPE OF CONTAINER (PLURAL) _____

NUMBER _____

PLURAL NOUN _____

ANOTHER PLURAL NOUN _____

ADJECTIVE _____

TYPE OF FOOD _____

ANOTHER TYPE OF FOOD _____

VERB (PAST TENSE) _____

NOUN _____

TYPE OF FOOD (PLURAL) _____

ANOTHER TYPE OF FOOD (PLURAL) _____

ADJECTIVE _____

ADVERB _____

MAD LIBS®
WHAT'S FOR DINNER, SCOOBY-DOO?

"So, Shaggy," said Daphne _____, "what should we buy at
                                 ADVERB

the _____ store this week?" "Hmmm," Shaggy answered,
         NOUN

"we're almost out of _____, and I know Scooby-Doo
                           PLURAL NOUN

finished all the _____ the other night while we were
                  TYPE OF FOOD (PLURAL)

_____. Shaggy started to look in the cabinets and in the
VERB ENDING IN "ING"

_____. He found _____ _____ but no
TYPE OF CONTAINER (PLURAL)   NUMBER   PLURAL NOUN

_____, not even a/an _____ crumb. "I think we
ANOTHER PLURAL NOUN   ADJECTIVE

need to go to the grocery store and stock up on _____ and
                                                 TYPE OF FOOD

_____," he told Daphne. "Scooby has _____
ANOTHER TYPE OF FOOD   VERB (PAST TENSE)

us out of house and _____!" So they went shopping and filled
                         NOUN

the van with _____ and _____.
              TYPE OF FOOD (PLURAL)   ANOTHER TYPE OF FOOD (PLURAL)

"Well, that should be enough for a/an _____ dinner, but
                                          ADJECTIVE

we're going to have to come back tomorrow for more!" Shaggy said,

laughing _____.
          ADVERB

MAD LIBS® is fun to play with friends, but you can also play it by yourself! To begin with, DO NOT look at the story on the page below. Fill in the blanks on this page with the words called for. Then, using the words you have selected, fill in the blank spaces in the story.

Now you've created your own hilarious MAD LIBS® game!

THE MYSTERY MACHINE MYSTERY, PART 1

A PLACE _____

NUMBER _____

PLURAL NOUN _____

ANOTHER PLURAL NOUN_____

TYPE OF BUILDING _____

ROOM _____

ADJECTIVE_____

TYPE OF BUSINESS_____

ADJECTIVE_____

ADJECTIVE_____

PLURAL NOUN _____

VERB _____

SAME ROOM_____

One day, the gang decided they wanted to go on a trip to _____ .

A PLACE

Since they would be away for _____ days, they packed suitcases

NUMBER

filled with _____ and _____ . On the day they

PLURAL NOUN ANOTHER PLURAL NOUN

were going to leave, they went to get the Mystery Machine from the

_____ . But, when they got inside, the van was missing!

TYPE OF BUILDING

They looked in the _____ , in the _____ street and even at the

ROOM ADJECTIVE

local _____ , but the Mystery Machine was nowhere to

TYPE OF BUSINESS

be found. "This is very _____ ," said Velma. "I think we have a

ADJECTIVE

mystery to solve, don't you?" Daphne nodded. "This might be the work

of _____ villains, so we should start looking for _____ ."

ADJECTIVE PLURAL NOUN

Fred and Velma started to _____ around the _____

VERB SAME ROOM

but couldn't discover anything about what happened to the Mystery

Machine.

From *Scooby-Doo™ Mystery Mad Libs®* • SCOOBY-DOO and all related characters
and elements are trademarks of Hanna-Barbera © 2003. Mad Libs® format copyright © 2003
by Price Stern Sloan, a division of Penguin Putnam Books for Young Readers.

MAD LIBS® is fun to play with friends, but you can also play it by yourself! To begin with, DO NOT look at the story on the page below. Fill in the blanks on this page with the words called for. Then, using the words you have selected, fill in the blank spaces in the story.

Now you've created your own hilarious MAD LIBS® game!

THE MYSTERY MACHINE
MYSTERY, PART 2

ADJECTIVE_____

VERB (PAST TENSE)_____

ADJECTIVE_____

ADVERB_____

NOUN _____

A PLACE _____

ADJECTIVE_____

NUMBER _____

ADJECTIVE_____

TYPE OF LIQUID _____

MAD LIBS®
THE MYSTERY MACHINE
MYSTERY, PART 2

The Mystery Machine was still _____ , so everyone went back
                                    ADJECTIVE

to the house to find Scooby-Doo and Shaggy. "We have a problem,"

Velma told Scooby. "The Mystery Machine has been _____ .
                                           VERB (PAST TENSE)

We have to do something _____!" Fred started to explain
                                  ADJECTIVE

about how they had been searching _____ all morning for the
                                      ADVERB

_____ and to tell them about how they needed it to go on their
NOUN

vacation to _____ . As Fred and Velma were telling their side
                  A PLACE

of the story, Shaggy came along. "Like, why is everyone so upset?" he

wanted to know. "What's going on?" Daphne explained that the

Mystery Machine was _____ , and Fred told Shaggy that they
                             ADJECTIVE

had been looking for the Mystery Machine for over _____ hours
                                          NUMBER

already. "Whoa—there's no need to get _____," Shaggy said.
                                    ADJECTIVE

"I thought I could help out, and I took the Mystery Machine to the

service station to get filled up with _____! We're all ready
                                 TYPE OF LIQUID

to go!"

From *Scooby-Doo™ Mystery Mad Libs®* • SCOOBY-DOO and all related characters
and elements are trademarks of Hanna-Barbera © 2003. Mad Libs® format copyright © 2003
by Price Stern Sloan, a division of Penguin Putnam Books for Young Readers.

MAD LIBS® is fun to play with friends, but you can also play it by yourself! To begin with, DO NOT look at the story on the page below. Fill in the blanks on this page with the words called for. Then, using the words you have selected, fill in the blank spaces in the story.

Now you've created your own hilarious MAD LIBS® game!

THE SAFARI MYSTERY, PART 1

A PLACE _____

NOUN _____

ANIMAL (PLURAL) _____

ANOTHER ANIMAL (PLURAL)_____

ADJECTIVE_____

SAME PLACE_____

VEHICLE _____

SILLY WORD_____

PLURAL NOUN _____

OCCUPATION _____

SAME VEHICLE_____

PLURAL NOUN _____

ADJECTIVE_____

VERB _____

SAME VEHICLE_____

VERB _____

ADJECTIVE _____

Daphne decided that the gang should take a trip to _____,
<u>A PLACE</u>

in Africa, for a _____ safari. She wanted to see all the wild
<u>NOUN</u>

_____ and _____ before they became
<u>ANIMAL (PLURAL)</u> <u>ANOTHER ANIMAL (PLURAL)</u>

_____. When they got to _____, they joined a tour
<u>ADJECTIVE</u> <u>SAME PLACE</u>

that was going to take a _____ down the _____ River.
<u>VEHICLE</u> <u>SILLY WORD</u>

They were hoping to be able to see lots of _____ in their
<u>PLURAL NOUN</u>

natural environment. Their tour guide was none other than Dr. Joan

Goodfew, the world-famous _____. As the gang was getting
<u>OCCUPATION</u>

their luggage onto the _____, they heard a strange noise that
<u>SAME VEHICLE</u>

sounded like wild _____. As they looked around them,
<u>PLURAL NOUN</u>

they saw that a herd of _____ glowing animals had started to
<u>ADJECTIVE</u>

_____ around the _____. "Run—before the
<u>VERB</u> <u>SAME VEHICLE</u>

animals can _____! Beware of the demon animals!" the
<u>VERB</u>

_____ guides said, as they ran into the jungle. Fred
<u>ADJECTIVE</u>

turned to look for Dr. Goodfew, but she had disappeared.

MAD LIBS® is fun to play with friends, but you can also play it by yourself! To begin with, DO NOT look at the story on the page below. Fill in the blanks on this page with the words called for. Then, using the words you have selected, fill in the blank spaces in the story.

Now you've created your own hilarious MAD LIBS® game!

THE SAFARI MYSTERY, PART 2

NUMBER _____

ADJECTIVE_____

NOUN _____

ADJECTIVE_____

PLURAL NOUN _____

ADJECTIVE_____

PLURAL NOUN _____

OCCUPATION (PLURAL) _____

VERB _____

PLURAL NOUN _____

VERB _____

PLURAL NOUN _____

ADJECTIVE _____

MAD LIBS®
THE SAFARI MYSTERY, PART 2

The gang was surrounded by _____ of the _____ animals,
      NUMBER   ADJECTIVE

and Dr. Goodfew was gone. "Like, this seems like a real _____ to
                  NOUN

me," said Shaggy. "I think you are _____," Daphne said. "We
           ADJECTIVE

should be on the lookout for _____." But before they could
         PLURAL NOUN

start looking, Dr. Goodfew returned. "What is going on with these

_____ animals?" Velma asked. Dr. Goodfew explained that the
ADJECTIVE

spirits of the _____ in the jungle were angry and trying to
     PLURAL NOUN

drive away all of the living creatures. "Too many _____
               OCCUPATION (PLURAL)

have moved into the area, and they are angering the spirits," she said.

"We must leave before they _____!" Everyone had loaded their
          VERB

_____ and they were about to _____ when the sound of
PLURAL NOUN   VERB

the _____ in the jungle started to get _____. "Zoinks!"
  PLURAL NOUN   ADJECTIVE

said Shaggy. "Like, I have a bad feeling about this!"

MAD LIBS® is fun to play with friends, but you can also play it by yourself! To begin with, DO NOT look at the story on the page below. Fill in the blanks on this page with the words called for. Then, using the words you have selected, fill in the blank spaces in the story.

Now you've created your own hilarious MAD LIBS® game!

THE SAFARI MYSTERY, PART 3

VERB _____

ADJECTIVE _____

PLURAL NOUN _____

PLURAL NOUN _____

ADJECTIVE _____

PLURAL NOUN _____

VERB _____

VERB ENDING IN "ING" _____

SAME VEHICLE AS IN PART 2 _____

ADVERB _____

SAME VEHICLE _____

VERB _____

NOUN _____

SAME NOUN _____

VERB _____

PLURAL NOUN _____

ADJECTIVE _____

ADJECTIVE _____

As night started to _____ , everyone could hear the sounds of

VERB

the _____ animals coming closer and closer. They could see

ADJECTIVE

phantom _____ gathering on the shores of the river and

PLURAL NOUN

ghostly _____ moving through the trees. Scooby-Doo and

PLURAL NOUN

Shaggy had an idea—they would scare the animals away by making

_____ noises. First, they got everyone to make the sounds of

ADJECTIVE

_____ , then they started to _____ the horn, but it didn't

PLURAL NOUN ___ VERB

work. Just then Velma saw Dr. Goodfew, _____ at the

VERB ENDING IN "ING"

back of the _____ . "I think I know the answer to this

SAME VEHICLE AS IN PART 2

jungle mystery," Velma said. She _____ walked to the back of the

ADVERB

_____ and started to _____ . "Dr. Goodfew," she said, "I

SAME VEHICLE ___ VERB

know what you're up to!" Dr. Goodfew came forward holding a giant

_____ in her hands. "You've been using a remote control _____

NOUN ___ SAME NOUN

to control the animals and scare off tourists, haven't you?" Dr. Good-

few started to _____ as she replied, "You tourists are ruining my

VERB

precious Africa. All of the _____ in the area belong to me, and

PLURAL NOUN

I did what I had to do. I would have gotten away with everything if

it weren't for you _____ kids and your _____ dog!"

ADJECTIVE ___ ADJECTIVE

MAD LIBS® is fun to play with friends, but you can also play it by yourself! To begin with, DO NOT look at the story on the page below. Fill in the blanks on this page with the words called for. Then, using the words you have selected, fill in the blank spaces in the story.

Now you've created your own hilarious MAD LIBS® game!

THE CASE OF THE
MISSING SCOOBY SNACKS

VERB ENDING IN "ING" _____

TYPE OF FOOD _____

ADVERB _____

NOUN _____

ANOTHER NOUN _____

PLURAL NOUN _____

SAME TYPE OF FOOD _____

ADJECTIVE _____

VERB _____

TYPE OF LIQUID _____

PART OF THE BODY _____

VERB (PAST TENSE) _____

ADJECTIVE _____

MAD LIBS®
THE CASE OF THE
MISSING SCOOBY SNACKS

One day, Scooby-Doo was _____ around his house and
VERB ENDING IN "ING"

watching TV. Before his favorite program started, Scooby went into the

kitchen to get a snack. When he opened the cabinet, he discovered

that his last box of _____ snacks had _____ disappeared.
TYPE OF FOOD   ADVERB

He looked everywhere—in the _____ , under the _____
NOUN   ANOTHER NOUN

and even between the _____ on the sofa. There were no
PLURAL NOUN

_____ snacks anywhere! Scooby was sure it was the
SAME TYPE OF FOOD

the work of a/an _____ villain. He was so sad, he started to
ADJECTIVE

_____ uncontrollably. _____ streamed down his face,
VERB   TYPE OF LIQUID

and his whole _____ was shaking. Just then Daphne
PART OF THE BODY

entered the room. "Scooby-Doo, what happened to you?" she said.

"Ro rore Rooby Racks," he said, sobbing. "Don't you remember, you

_____ them last night. I just came back from the store
VERB (PAST TENSE)

with a whole _____ case of them for you."
ADJECTIVE

MAD LIBS® is fun to play with friends, but you can also play it by yourself! To begin with, DO NOT look at the story on the page below. Fill in the blanks on this page with the words called for. Then, using the words you have selected, fill in the blank spaces in the story.

Now you've created your own hilarious MAD LIBS® game!

LIGHTS, CAMERA, SCOOBY!, PART 1

SILLY WORD _____

PLURAL NOUN _____

OCCUPATION _____

ANOTHER OCCUPATION _____

ADJECTIVE _____

SAME PLURAL NOUN _____

ADVERB _____

ADJECTIVE _____

ADVERB _____

NUMBER _____

VERB ENDING IN "S" _____

PLURAL NOUN _____

NOUN _____

MAD LIBS®
LIGHTS, CAMERA, SCOOBY!, PART 1

The gang had been invited to visit _____ Studios for a tour.
<u>SILLY WORD</u>

It was very exciting. They were able to see the set of "Attack of the

_____," a new action/adventure movie by the famous
<u>PLURAL NOUN</u>

_____ Vincent Wong. They were even going to meet a real-
<u>OCCUPATION</u>

live _____ . "Like, wow!" Shaggy said. "We get to
<u>ANOTHER OCCUPATION</u>

meet Chip Hernandez, Jr., the _____ star of this movie!" Vincent
<u>ADJECTIVE</u>

took them on a tour of the set, but Chip was nowhere in sight. Vincent

had an idea to fill the time until Chip arrived. "You can help me. I

need some people to be my stunt doubles since we've already spent

our entire budget on _____ . We can't afford to hire any-
<u>SAME PLURAL NOUN</u>

one new," Vincent said _____ . "Are you interested?" "You bet! We're
<u>ADVERB</u>

_____ !" said Fred. "That's great," Vincent said _____ . "But first
<u>ADJECTIVE</u>   <u>ADVERB</u>

there is something I have to warn you about. For _____ weeks,
<u>NUMBER</u>

the set has been haunted by a phantom. He _____ in
<u>VERB ENDING IN "S"</u>

from nowhere, messes up our _____ and then vanishes.
<u>PLURAL NOUN</u>

I don't know what to do," Vincent said. "This _____ could ruin
<u>NOUN</u>

our production!"

MAD LIBS® is fun to play with friends, but you can also play it by yourself! To begin with, DO NOT look at the story on the page below. Fill in the blanks on this page with the words called for. Then, using the words you have selected, fill in the blank spaces in the story.

Now you've created your own hilarious MAD LIBS® game!

LIGHTS, CAMERA, SCOOBY!, PART 2

ADJECTIVE _____

NOUN _____

VERB ENDING IN "ING" _____

ADJECTIVE _____

ADJECTIVE _____

NOUN _____

COLOR _____

ARTICLE OF CLOTHING (PLURAL) _____

OCCUPATION (PLURAL) _____

ADJECTIVE _____

ADVERB _____

ANOTHER ARTICLE OF CLOTHING _____

PART OF THE BODY _____

NOUN _____

ANOTHER PART OF THE BODY _____

NOUN _____

NOUN _____

ADJECTIVE _____

"This phantom sounds _____," said Velma. "We found our-
ADJECTIVE

selves a _____ to solve!" "Someone must really want to stop
NOUN

_____ on this movie, but who?" asked Daphne. The
VERB ENDING IN "ING"

easiest way to find the clues was to just act _____. They
ADJECTIVE

began getting into their costumes. Fred put on a/an _____ hat
ADJECTIVE

that made him look like a/an _____. Shaggy and Scooby wore
NOUN

_____ _____, and the girls decided to
COLOR   ARTICLE OF CLOTHING (PLURAL)

dress as _____. Just then, they heard a/an _____
OCCUPATION (PLURAL)   ADJECTIVE

noise coming from the back of the costume shop. "Oh, no! It's the

phantom!" Victor said _____. The phantom came closer and
ADVERB

closer. He was wearing a tattered _____ and had
ANOTHER ARTICLE OF CLOTHING

a _____ that looked like a/an _____. He was waving
PART OF THE BODY   NOUN

his _____ in the air and making sounds just like
ANOTHER PART OF THE BODY

a broken _____, and then he vanished. "Where is Chip? We
NOUN

should protect him from the _____," Shaggy said. "We haven't
NOUN

seen him in a while, and I'm starting to get _____!"
ADJECTIVE

MAD LIBS® is fun to play with friends, but you can also play it by yourself! To begin with, DO NOT look at the story on the page below. Fill in the blanks on this page with the words called for. Then, using the words you have selected, fill in the blank spaces in the story.

Now you've created your own hilarious MAD LIBS® game!

LIGHTS, CAMERA, SCOOBY!, PART 3

VERB _____

NOUN _____

VERB ENDING IN "ING" _____

ROOM _____

PLURAL NOUN _____

ANOTHER ROOM _____

ANOTHER ROOM _____

VERB ENDING IN "ING" _____

NOUN _____

ADVERB _____

NUMBER _____

SILLY WORD _____

NOUN _____

The gang decided that they needed to find Chip and _____ as

VERB

soon as they could. It just wasn't safe for a _____ anymore

NOUN

around the studio, not with a phantom _____ around.

VERB ENDING IN "ING"

So they split into groups to search the lot. Shaggy and Scooby headed

for the _____—hoping they could find some _____

ROOM _PLURAL NOUN_

to snack on while they looked. Fred and Vincent started looking in

the _____, and Velma and Daphne went straight for the

ANOTHER ROOM

_____. But Chip was nowhere to be found! When the

ANOTHER ROOM

group met up again, they still hadn't figured out why the phantom

was trying to keep them from _____ and finishing

VERB ENDING IN "ING"

the movie. "If we don't solve the _____ soon," said Vincent

NOUN

_____, "we're going to have to halt production. We'll lose over

ADVERB

_____ dollars, and my name will be _____. I won't be

NUMBER _SILLY WORD_

able to make even a/an _____ in Hollywood ever again."

NOUN

From *Scooby-Doo™ Mystery Mad Libs®* • SCOOBY-DOO and all related characters
and elements are trademarks of Hanna-Barbera © 2003. Mad Libs® format copyright © 2003
by Price Stern Sloan, a division of Penguin Putnam Books for Young Readers.

MAD LIBS® is fun to play with friends, but you can also play it by yourself! To begin with, DO NOT look at the story on the page below. Fill in the blanks on this page with the words called for. Then, using the words you have selected, fill in the blank spaces in the story.

Now you've created your own hilarious MAD LIBS® game!

LIGHTS, CAMERA, SCOOBY!, PART 4

ADJECTIVE_____

SILLY WORD_____

NAME OF PERSON IN ROOM_____

ADJECTIVE_____

ADVERB_____

PLURAL NOUN_____

PART OF THE BODY_____

ARTICLE OF CLOTHING_____

VERB ENDING IN "ING"_____

SAME NAME_____

OCCUPATION_____

ANOTHER OCCUPATION_____

ADJECTIVE_____

MAD LIBS®
LIGHTS, CAMERA, SCOOBY!, PART 4

"I think that's it," Velma said. "This has to do with Chip Hernandez.

Didn't I read in _____ Hollywood Magazine that Chip was
            ADJECTIVE

interested in working on ' _____ ,' that hot new movie
                              SILLY WORD

directed by _____? It's supposed to start filming
            NAME OF PERSON IN ROOM

next week." Just then, they heard a/an _____ thump from the
                                         ADJECTIVE

back of the room. "The phantom!" said Shaggy _____ . "Like,
                                                 ADVERB

run for your _____ !" Scooby started running, but he ran
             PLURAL NOUN

towards the phantom and knocked him off of his _____ .
                                                 PART OF THE BODY

The gang gathered around and removed the _____
                                          ARTICLE OF CLOTHING

that the phantom was wearing. Sure enough, Chip Hernandez was

_____ underneath. "Why did you do it, Chip?" asked
VERB ENDING IN "ING"

Vincent. "I wanted the chance to work with _____ . He/She
                                             SAME NAME

could have helped me be a really great _____ , not just a teen
                                          OCCUPATION

_____," Chip explained. "I would have gotten away
ANOTHER OCCUPATION

with it, too, if it weren't for Scooby-Doo and his _____ friends!"
                                                    ADJECTIVE

MAD LIBS® is fun to play with friends, but you can also play it by yourself! To begin with, DO NOT look at the story on the page below. Fill in the blanks on this page with the words called for. Then, using the words you have selected, fill in the blank spaces in the story.

Now you've created your own hilarious MAD LIBS® game!

MYSTERY ON THE ORIENT EXPRESS, PART 1

ADJECTIVE_____

VEHICLE _____

A PLACE _____

ANOTHER PLACE _____

NUMBER _____

NUMBER _____

PLURAL NOUN _____

ADJECTIVE_____

PLURAL NOUN _____

PLURAL NOUN _____

SAME VEHICLE_____

PLURAL NOUN _____

ADJECTIVE_____

Scooby-Doo and the gang were invited to take a trip on the famous,

_____ Orient Express. It was a/an _____ that traveled from
  ADJECTIVE   VEHICLE

_____ to _____ at a speed of over _____ miles
  A PLACE   ANOTHER PLACE   NUMBER

per hour. It was very exciting. The trip would take _____ days.
                                                       NUMBER

When they got on board, everyone was assigned to their cabins,

which are also called "_____." Shaggy and Fred would
                              PLURAL NOUN

share a cabin with Scooby, while Daphne and Velma would be in an-

other one across the corridor. "It's going to be very _____ to
                                                        ADJECTIVE

take a trip without having any _____ to solve," said Velma.
                                   PLURAL NOUN

"We can act just like we are regular _____." However, she
                                        PLURAL NOUN

spoke too soon. Even though it was late and the _____ was
                                                    SAME VEHICLE

traveling between two _____, all of a sudden, the Orient
                          PLURAL NOUN

Express came to a/an _____ halt.
                        ADJECTIVE

MAD LIBS® is fun to play with friends, but you can also play it by yourself! To begin with, DO NOT look at the story on the page below. Fill in the blanks on this page with the words called for. Then, using the words you have selected, fill in the blank spaces in the story.

Now you've created your own hilarious MAD LIBS® game!

MYSTERY ON THE ORIENT EXPRESS, PART 2

PART OF THE BODY (PLURAL) _____

OCCUPATION (PLURAL) _____

VERB _____

ADVERB_____

ADJECTIVE_____

PLURAL NOUN _____

SAME VEHICLE AS IN PART 1 _____

OCCUPATION _____

NOUN _____

PLURAL NOUN _____

ADJECTIVE_____

ANIMAL _____

VERB ENDING IN "ING" _____

SAME VEHICLE_____

SAME ANIMAL _____

VERB _____

TYPE OF FOOD _____

PLURAL NOUN _____

VERB ENDING IN "ING" _____

"Whoa!" yelled Shaggy. "Like, what happened?" Daphne stuck her

_____ out in the corridor and looked around. "I
PART OF THE BODY (PLURAL)

don't see any _____ . Maybe we should _____
OCCUPATION (PLURAL)   VERB

and see what we can find," she said _____ . "This could be a/an
ADVERB

_____ mystery after all." The gang split up to look for _____ .
ADJECTIVE   PLURAL NOUN

Daphne and Velma went to the front of the _____
SAME VEHICLE AS IN PART 1

to talk to its _____ . Fred went towards the back of the
OCCUPATION

_____ to see if he could find any _____ . "And we'll
NOUN   PLURAL NOUN

go to the dining car to find a/an _____ snack!" said Shaggy.
ADJECTIVE

They solved the mystery in no time at all. The girls learned that there

was a/an _____ _____ on the tracks, and
ANIMAL   VERB ENDING IN "ING"

the _____ was stuck until the _____ rancher
SAME VEHICLE   SAME ANIMAL

arrived. There was nothing to do but _____ . "And there's
VERB

plenty of time for a snack of _____ and _____ ,"
TYPE OF FOOD   PLURAL NOUN

Shaggy said, as the gang got back together in the _____
VERB ENDING IN "ING"

car. "Scooby-dooby-doo!" said Scooby.